Yes We Can!

for Felix
C.F.

Originally published in Great Britain by Puffin Books

ISBN-13: 978-0-545-11163-8
ISBN-10: 0-545-11163-3

12 11 10 9 8 7 6 5 4 3 2 1   8 9 10 11 12 13/0

Printed in the U.S.A.   08

First Scholastic printing, September 2008

Yes We Can!

Sam McBratney & Charles Fuge

SCHOLASTIC INC.

New York Toronto London Auckland Sydney
Mexico City New Delhi Hong Kong Buenos Aires

Little Roo was chasing leaves one windy day.
Roo's friends, Country Mouse
and Quacker Duck, were waiting
to play with him.

"Let's make a big pile of leaves," said Roo.
"A mountain of leaves," said Country Mouse.
"The biggest ever seen!" quacked Duck.

They began to collect up all the leaves they could find
but making a leaf mountain is hard work,
so after a while they stopped for a rest.

While they were resting, Little Roo
said to his friend Quacker Duck,
"I know something you can't do.
You can't jump over a big, big log."

"Yes I can,"

said Quacker Duck.

Quacker Duck tried as hard
as she could,
but little ducks aren't
made to jump over
big, big logs.

Country Mouse thought it was
so funny when Quacker Duck
fell over the fallen-down tree.

"Don't you laugh at me!" said Quacker Duck to Country Mouse. "I know something you can't do. You can't float on a puddle."

"Yes I can," said Country Mouse.

So Country Mouse tried to float
on the puddle . . .

but a little mouse isn't
really made for
f l o a t i n g.

Little Roo thought it was **so** funny
when Country Mouse crawled out of the water,
soaking wet
and dripping.

"Don't you laugh at me!"
said Country Mouse.
"I know something you can't do.
You can't catch your own tail."

"Yes I can,"

said Roo.

Roo tried as hard as he could
to **catch** his own tail,
but his tail would **not**
be caught.

It was too **far** away.

Country Mouse
and Quacker Duck
laughed and **laughed**
as Roo ran around
in circles.

"Don't you **dare** laugh at me!" cried Roo.
"Well, **you** laughed at me!" said Mouse.
"And **you** laughed at me!" said Duck.

No one
was
happy.

No one was happy because each
had made fun of someone else
and someone else had made fun of them.

Instead of making the biggest mountain
of leaves that anyone had ever seen, they
looked as if they might all go home in a
bad mood.

Little Roo's mother came over
to see what the fuss was about.
"I'm not surprised the three of
you look so grumpy," she said.
"Nobody likes to be
laughed at!"

It was true.
No one likes to be laughed at.
"Why don't you show each other
what you **can** do?" said Roo's mom.

Roo cried, "I can jump over a big, big log!"

He hopped **up** and **over** the fallen-down tree.

"That's **really** good **jumping**,"
the others said.

"I can float on a puddle," said Quacker Duck,
taking to the water with ease.

"That's really excellent floating!"
the others agreed.

And when Country Mouse caught his own tail,
Little Roo and Quacker Duck
thought that his
tail-catching was
the best they had
ever seen.

"There now," said Roo's mother,
  "can we all be friends again?"
Little Roo, Country Mouse, and
  Quacker Duck looked at one another.
They were all thinking the same thing . . .

"Yes we can!"